PUFFIN BOOKS

THE LITTLE GIRL AND
THE TINY DOLL

There was once a tiny doll who belonged to a girl who did not care for dolls. One day when the little girl was shopping in the super-market with her mother, she threw the tiny doll into a deep freeze.

So the tiny doll had to stay there, cold and lonely, and fright-ened by people shuffling all the food round her. But someone came along who felt sorry for her, and thought of ways to make her happier, so the tiny doll began to smile again.

Edward and Aingelda Ardizzone have produced a delightful tale which will be enjoyed by young children as a story to be read to them or by older children beginning to read for themselves.

Edward Ardizzone was born in 1900, the eldest of five children. He took a number of clerical jobs, then attended evening classes at the Westminster School of Art, and became a professional painter. Several of his pictures have been bought by the Tate Gallery. During World War II he was one of the six official war artists. He illustrated about 200 books and was awarded the Kate Greenaway Medal for *Tim All Alone*. He was awarded the C.B.E. in 1971. He died in 1979.

Aingelda Ardizzone is Edward Ardizzone's daughter-in-law and lives on a pretty village green in Kent. She has five children, to whom she originally told this story. She studied at the Slade School of Fine Art, and is a painter of landscapes.

EDWARD AND AINGELDA
ARDIZZONE

THE LITTLE GIRL
AND THE TINY DOLL

PUFFIN BOOKS

PUFFIN BOOKS

Published by the Penguin Group
Penguin Books Ltd, 27 Wrights Lane, London W8 5TZ, England
Penguin Books USA Inc., 375 Hudson Street, New York, New York 10014, USA
Penguin Books Australia Ltd, Ringwood, Victoria, Australia
Penguin Books Canada Ltd, 2801 John Street, Markham, Ontario, Canada L3R 1B4
Penguin Books (NZ) Ltd, 182–190 Wairau Road, Auckland 10, New Zealand

Penguin Books Ltd, Registered Offices: Harmondsworth, Middlesex, England

First published in Great Britain by Longman Young Books 1966
This edition published in Puffin Books 1979
9 10

Printed in England by Clays Ltd, St Ives plc
Set in Monotype Baskerville

To Miss Irene Theobald

There was once a tiny doll who
belonged to a girl who did not care
for dolls so her life was very dull.

For a long time she lay forgotten
in a mackintosh pocket until one
rainy day when the girl was out
shopping.

The girl was following her
mother round a grocer's shop
when she put her hand in

her pocket and felt something
hard. She took it out and saw it
was the doll.

'Ugly old thing,' she said and
quickly put it back again, as she
thought, into her pocket.

But, in fact, it fell unnoticed into the deep freeze container among the frozen peas.

The tiny doll lay quite still for a long time,

wondering what was to become of her.

She felt so sad, partly because
she did not like being called ugly
and partly because she was lost.

It was very cold in the deep freeze
and the tiny doll began to feel rather
stiff, so she decided to walk about
and have a good look at the place.

The floor was crisp and white
just like frost on a winter's morning.

There were many packets of peas
piled one on top of the other.
They seemed to her like great big
buildings. The cracks between the
piles were rather like narrow
streets.

She walked one way and then the
other, passing, not only packets of
peas, but packets of sliced beans,
spinach, broccoli and mixed
vegetables. Then she turned a corner

and found herself among beef rissoles
and fish fingers. However, she did not
stop but went on exploring until she
came to boxes of strawberries; and
then ice-cream.

The strawberries reminded her of
the time when she was lost once
before among the strawberry plants
in a garden.

Then she sat all day in the sun
smelling and eating strawberries.

Now she made herself as
comfortable as possible.

But it was not easy as the
customers kept taking boxes out to
buy them

and the shop people would put new
ones in and not always very carefully,
either.

At times it was quite frightening.
Once she was nearly squashed by a
box of fish fingers.

The tiny doll had no idea how
long she spent in the deep freeze.

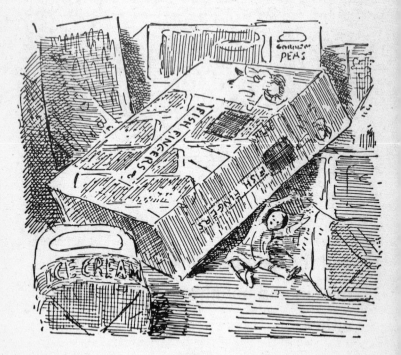

Sometimes it seemed very quiet.
This, she supposed, was when the
shop was closed for the night.

She could not keep count of the
days.

One day when she was busy
eating ice-cream out of a packet,
she suddenly looked up and saw a
little girl she had never seen before.

The little girl was sorry for the tiny
doll and longed to take her home
to be with her other dolls.

The doll looked so cold and lonely,
but the girl did not dare to pick
her up because she had been told
not to touch things in the shop.

However, she felt she must do
something to help the doll and as
soon as she got home she set to
work to make her some warm clothes.

First of all, she made her a warm
bonnet out of a piece of red flannel.
This was a nice and easy thing to
start with.

After tea that day she asked mother
to help her cut out a coat from a
piece of blue velvet.

She stitched away so hard that
she had just time to finish it before
she went to bed.

It was very beautiful.

The next day her mother said they were going shopping, so the little girl put the coat and bonnet in an empty matchbox and tied it into a neat parcel with brown paper and string.

She held the parcel tightly in her
hand as she walked along the
street, hurrying as she went. She
longed to know if the tiny doll
would still be there.

As soon as she reached the shop
she ran straight to the deep freeze
to look for her.

At first she could not see her anywhere.
Then, suddenly, she saw her, right
at the back, playing with the peas.

The tiny doll was throwing them
into the air and hitting them with
an ice-cream spoon.

It was a very dull game but it was
something to do.

The little girl threw in the parcel and the doll at once started to untie it.

She looked very pleased when she saw what was inside.

She tried on the coat, and it fitted.
She tried on the bonnet and it fitted
too. She was very pleased.

She jumped up and down with
excitement and waved to the little
girl to say thank you.

She felt so much better in warm clothes and it made her feel happy to think that somebody cared for her.

Then she had an idea. She made the matchbox into a bed and pretended that the brown paper was a great big blanket.

With the string she wove a mat to go beside the bed.

At last she settled down in the matchbox, wrapped herself in the brown paper blanket and went to sleep.

She had a long, long sleep because she
was very tired and, when she woke up,
she found that the little girl had been

back again and had left another
parcel. This time it contained a yellow
scarf. She had always wanted a scarf.

Now the little girl came back to the shop every day and each time she brought something new for the tiny doll.

She made her
a sweater,

a petticoat,

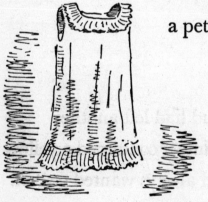

knickers with tiny frills,

and gave her a little bit of looking-glass to see herself in.

She also gave her some red tights
which belonged to one of her own
dolls to see if they would fit. They
fitted perfectly.

At last the tiny doll was beautifully
dressed and looked quite cheerful,
but still nobody except the little girl
ever noticed her.

'Couldn't we ask someone about the
doll?' the little girl asked her mother.
'I would love to take her home to
play with.'

The mother said she would ask
the lady at the cash desk when they
went to pay for their shopping.

46

'Do you know about the doll in the
deep freeze?'
'No, indeed,' the lady replied.
'There are no dolls in this shop.'

'Oh yes there are,' said the little
girl and her mother, both at once.

So the lady from the cash desk, the
little girl and her mother all marched

off to have a look,
And there, sure enough, was the
tiny doll down among the frozen peas,
looking cold and bored.

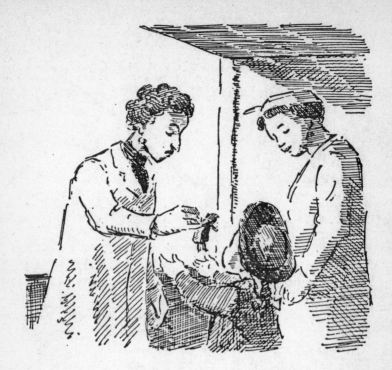

'It's not much of a life for a doll in
there,' said the shop lady picking up
the doll and giving it to the little girl.
'You had better take her home
where she will be out of mischief.'

Having said this, she marched back
to her desk with rather a haughty
expression.

The little girl took the tiny doll
home, where she lived for many
happy years in a beautiful doll's
house. The little girl loved her and
played with her a great deal.

But, best of all, she liked the company
of the other dolls, because they all
loved to listen to her stories about
the time when she lived in the deep
freeze.

THE END

Some other Young Puffins

THE RAILWAY CAT AND DIGBY
Phyllis Arkle

Further adventures of Alfie the railway cat, who always seems to be in Leading Railman Hack's bad books. Alfie is a smart cat, a lot smarter than many people think, and he would like to be friends with Hack. But when he tries to improve matters by 'helping' Hack's dog, Digby, to win a prize at the local show, the situation rapidly goes from bad to worse!

BURGLAR BELLS
John Escott

In horror, Bernie and Lee watch a man climbing through the window of an empty house. Is he a burglar? When news breaks out of a burglary in that road, the pair are convinced it was the man they saw – who is going to marry Miss Daisy, the charming school secretary. What should they do? Find out in this exciting, fast-moving adventure.

MR BERRY'S ICE-CREAM PARLOUR
Jennifer Zabel

Carl is thrilled when Mr Berry, the new lodger, comes to stay. But when Mr Berry announces his plan to open an ice-cream parlour, Carl can hardly believe it. And this is just the start of the excitement in store when Mr Berry walks through the door.

THE CONKER AS HARD AS A DIAMOND

Chris Powling

Last conker season little Alpesh had lost every single game, and that's why he's determined this year's going to be different. This year he's going to win, and he won't stop until he's Conker Champion of the Universe! The trouble is, only a conker as hard as a diamond will make it possible – and where on earth is he going to find one?

TALES FROM ALLOTMENT LANE SCHOOL

Margaret Joy

Twelve delightful stories, bright, light and funny, about the children in Miss Mee's class at Allotment Lane School. Meet Ian, the avid collector; meet Mary and Gary, who have busy mornings taking messages; and meet the school caterpillars, who disappear and turn up again in surprising circumstances.

THE PICTURE PRIZE
and Other Stories

Simon Watson

A picture competition in which Wallace gets paint into some very unusual places, an escaped horse which has to be taken home, magic chickens and great, hairy, striped caterpillars are just a few of the exciting things that come into Wallace's life.

MARGARET AND TAYLOR

Kevin Henkes

Seven simple stories featuring Margaret and Taylor, a brother and sister whose competitive relationship leads to lots of amusing and instantly familiar domestic incidents.

DINNER AT ALBERTA'S

Russell Hoban

Arthur the crocodile has extremely bad table manners until he is invited to dinner at Alberta's.

LITTLE DOG LOST

Nina Warner Hooke

The adventures of Pepito, a scruffy black and white puppy, who lives in an old soap-powder box in Spain. The excitement starts when the rubbish collectors sweep Pepito up in his box and deposit him at the bottom of a disused quarry, miles from anywhere! A touching and amusing tale.

TWO VILLAGE DINOSAURS

Phyllis Arkle

Two dinosaurs spell double trouble as Dino and Sauro trample their amiable way through the village, causing chaos and confusion on every side.

DORRIE AND THE BIRTHDAY EGGS
DORRIE AND THE HAUNTED HOUSE
DORRIE AND THE GOBLIN
DORRIE AND THE WIZARD'S SPELL

Patricia Coombs

A series of delightful books about the little witch, Dorrie, her cat Gink and her mother the Big Witch. They all live cheerfully together in a house with a tower and they have many exciting adventures.

THE DEAD LETTER BOX

Jan Mark

Louie's friend Glenda moves house and Louie arranges a 'dead' letter box in a book in the library. But Glenda is no letter writer and the end result is chaos in the library.

ALBERT ON THE FARM

Alison Jezard

Albert and Digger, the koala bear from Australia, have a wonderful holiday working on a farm. They meet all sorts of people and animals and do all kinds of exciting things, including milking a cow and learning to make butter.

PROFESSOR BRANESTAWM'S POCKET MOTOR CAR

Norman Hunter

Two Branestawm stories specially written for younger readers: the Professor's amazing genius for invention produces an inflatable car to solve parking problems, and an extremely clever letter-writing machine.

THE WORST WITCH STRIKES AGAIN

Jill Murphy

Summer term at Miss Cackle's Academy for Witches had just begun, and diaster-prone Mildred Hubble was in trouble again – all because the new girl, Enid Nightshade, wasn't as placid as she looked . . .

FIONA FINDS HER TONGUE

Diana Hendry

At home Fiona is a chatterbox, but whenever she goes out she just won't say a word. How she overcomes her shyness and 'finds her tongue' is told in this charming book.

THE THREE AND MANY WISHES OF JASON REID

Hazel Hutchins

Jason is eleven and a very good thinker, so when he is granted three wishes he is very wary indeed. After all, he knows what tangles happen in fairy stories!

THE GINGERBREAD MAN

David Wood

The successful musical play which delights children all over the world, is now presented as an entertaining story book for young readers.

ONE NIL

Tony Bradman

Dave Brown is mad about football, and when he learns that the England squad are to train at the local City ground he thinks up a brilliant plan to overcome his parents' objections and gets to the ground to see them. A very amusing story.

THE GHOST AT No. 13

Gyles Brandreth

Hamlet Brown's sister, Susan, is just too perfect. Everything she does is praised and Hamlet is in despair – until the ghost comes to stay for a holiday and helps him to find an exciting idea for his school project.

ZOZU THE ROBOT

Diana Carter

Rufus and Sarah find a tiny frightened little robot and his space capsule in their garden.